Honey's
Sexy Surprise

By
Kate Richards

~A Note from the Author~

Dear Reader,

Thank you for taking time to read my story. I hope you'll enjoy Honey's erotic adventure and let me know what you think!

Kate Richards
Katerichards09@gmail.com

Chapter One

A warm armful of Honey brought life to his boyo, as it did every morning. Mack's wife could raise the dead if she put her mind to it. His cock, nestled between her soft, round buttocks, hardened more with every passing moment. He buried his face in the sweet-smelling caramel-colored hair he'd always loved. As most of his friends complained about their lack of a sex life, Mack fought the urge to tell them the cure lay between Honey's silky smooth thighs. Her sweetly curving breasts and tiny waist drew his hands, his lips. Standing, she came just to his shoulder, a perfect fit in bed.

He worried about being enough for her.

She'd given up so much for him and the kids....

***

"Honey, wanna do it?"

Morning wood. If it weren't for nature's early a.m. gift, they wouldn't do it anymore at all. She glanced at the clock and almost said no. Again. Why did he seek her out when she had to get up in five minutes and make breakfast, get the kids ready for school...?

Mack's strong arms tightened around her, and her resolve faded. He nuzzled her with his stubbly cheek, raising goose bumps on her skin.

"Okay, but we have to be fast." He knows that.

Once, they had spent long evenings making passionate love, with enough foreplay for anyone. Or at least for her. But more and more often, all Mack looked for from her was the precious five minutes before their day began.

So, while they still made love four times a week, which her girlfriends all assured her rated pretty great for an old married couple, these rewarding encounters totaled approximately twenty minutes per week. Well, fifteen, for the three weekdays and maybe another ten for Sundays. So twenty-five. And the only guaranteed Big O on the weekends. Although he still managed to get her off in their hurried embrace at least two times out of three.

Why process averages while his erection poked her in the ass? You can take the underwriter out of the office, but.... "Ohhh."

Mack murmured low in her ear. He pulled her tight against him. Next he would...yep, he cupped her breast and nudged his knee between her thighs. She could predict within seconds the exact routine.

Taking care of their family burned up more energy than she ever knew she had. If he didn't totally do it for her anyway, she'd have put an end to his nonsense long before. But the big guy did...so he got away with it.

He urged her legs wider. If it's Friday, it must be doggy-style. And we're off. He left her breast behind, and his hand drifted down to stimulate her. Despite the routine, she grew wet, her breath shortened, and his dick slipped inside.

Within the required time, she crashed over the edge into waves of pleasure—lasting about sixty seconds before—

A pounding on the door heralded the arrival of their younger daughter. "Mommm, I'm hungry."

Mack rocked against her one final time with a groan and dropped away. "Like clockwork."

She rolled to the side of the bed, slipped her feet into slippers, grabbed her robe, and stumbled to standing. "Mom's coming." Once upon a time she'd showered, styled her hair, and dressed in designer ensembles for the office.

"When will those kids learn to feed themselves?" His grumble held none of the pleasure of moments earlier, echoing her own silent complaint.

She missed the afterglow.

But as she shuffled off to the kitchen to prepare a healthy breakfast and pack lunches for her brood and the grumbly bear, Honey smiled. She scrambled a few eggs and toasted some whole-grain bread, set juice and glasses on the table, and started the coffee brewing.

All the ordinary moments of the day, the things keeping her family moving. But while the trio blond heads bowed over their meal, Honey slipped to her desk in the corner and brought up email. She clicked on the tracking number and confirmed. Out for delivery.

"What's up, Honey?"

She jumped. "What?"

He dropped a kiss on her head. "Is my lunch ready?"

"On the counter." Like every morning.

"Thanks. Anything exciting going on today?"

She minimized the screen. "Oh, you know." He didn't...but he would soon enough.

"Everything okay?" She was kind of surprised he noticed her distraction, but touched. Honey spun her desk chair and wrapped her arms around his waist, burying her face in his warm, just-big-enough-to-be-comforting belly. Mack had gained some in their years together, but it did nothing to lessen his appeal for her. His red hair was combed back, still damp from the shower.

"Everything is fine, and thank you for asking."

"Okay." The big goon kissed her hair again, and she let him go. "Have a good day." He scooped up his lunch box and headed toward the door, off to spend his shift with grownups. With his partner. All day in the squad car with Sexy Sandy.

The woman should be a model instead of a cop. Not that she didn't trust Mack, but why couldn't he have been assigned someone a little less...blonde.

Honey's gaze darted back to the screen. The answer to all their worries would be delivered by the guys in brown. Appropriate for the item. Even if not one of them could compete with the erotic lure of the guy she made dinner for every night.

Ten minutes later, she'd walked the kids to the bus, waved while they left then raced back to begin the real work of the day. Waiting for the box.

Honey paced from the living room to the kitchen and back again, still in her robe and slippers. She didn't dare leave the house for fear the delivery would require a signature. Or maybe not be in such a "discreet" package as the site advertised. Her next-door neighbor would love reporting a purchase from a sex toy site to everyone at the neighborhood watch meeting. Bitch.

Honey didn't even want to take a shower until the item was safe in her possession.

She also couldn't focus on anything else. Her dull life needed something to liven it up.

She hadn't minded staying home while the kids were little—not most of the time. She and Mack had agreed in her hospital room as she'd kissed Bonnie's downy, newborn head. Her job lent itself to telecommuting. She could return to the marble and steel high-rise and her corner office when their children were in school. A few years. And it might be nice to spend time at home.

So she'd worked during naps and late at night while her family slumbered, struggling to keep up and missing promotions others gained by their presence in the office—even if her work surpassed theirs. Not a situation Miss Most-Likely-To-Succeed tolerated with much grace.

But since their youngest had entered kindergarten, Honey's presence mattered even more. Homework and teacher conferences, three kids who took turns with colds and tummy troubles...how could she go back to work and leave them to another's care? Lots of moms didn't have the options she did.

So she worked at home, in sweats or pajamas, maybe shorts and a tank top on a good day. She wondered why her husband showed any interest at all. But she planned to make a change. Today.

Honey fled back to the computer and brought up Sodom&Gomorrah.com. "Sex toys guaranteed to send you straight to hell."

She giggled and hit the bookmark for the particular item she'd ordered. If she couldn't make vice president for a while, maybe she could win the award for most creative wife.

When her local friends offered no help with her problems—in fact seemed appalled a woman with such an active sex life would complain—Honey had consulted the her online acquaintances at HardworkingMoms.com. More and more often, these ladies who lived all over the world filled in the blanks where her PTA people left her flat. They seemed to understand her need for a life beyond wife and mother.

They were all stay at home moms like her, but they also found time and ways to express their creativity, their intelligence, and their sexuality. A resource she found invaluable—and kept secret from her other, daytime world. Even Mack.

Jenna from Belgium directed her to Sodom&Gomorrah.com, swearing their products saved her marriage to her US serviceman husband. Honey had clicked right to the site. She'd scanned page after page of toys in wide-eyed amazement. Vibrators of all sizes, shapes, and colors. Dildos. Bondage equipment from silken ropes to suspension harnesses. She considered a two-headed glass monster guaranteed to bring pleasure to both man and woman at the same time, but feared Mack would run screaming when he saw it. Or die laughing.

What she chose would have to be something he might find fascinating yet not terrifying.

After she selected and rejected half a dozen items, an ornate purple box appeared on her screen. Half price, today only.

Before she could lose her nerve, Honey placed the order and hit Send.

Two weeks later, she sat down to look at the item again.

Chapter Two

"Sandy, you're a woman."

Mack's partner kept her eyes on the road. "Yes, so?" Her tone held a warning. He puzzled a moment then plunged on.

"So...I don't understand my wife."

Sandy hit the brakes, hard. Squealing and honking came from behind them, but she ignored it, turning a reddened face to him. "How original. But you have it backwards, partner. The line is 'My wife doesn't understand me.'" Slamming a hand on the steering wheel, she jerked the car back into motion. "What the hell. I thought you were different. Not like those jerks at the precinct, always hitting on me and making one double entendre after another, thinking they are so clever."

Mack's jaw dropped in horror. "No. I'm not hitting on you. I mean what I said. I don't understand her. You've met Honey. She's bright and beautiful and smart. What does she want with a guy like me?"

A little smile quirked the edge of Sandy's mouth and she relaxed her grip on the wheel. "Sorry. For a moment, you had me going. I swear, someday that obnoxious jerk Baxter is going to say something offensive to me and I'm going to knock his block off. I can't believe such a letch is part of the force. The other guys are a little off-color, but nothing I can't take."

"You get violent, you'll wreck your career. Maybe you should talk to the chief."

"And have him lecture them all on sexual harassment? Since Juanita and I are the only women on the force, and she's at least sixty, everyone would know who complained. I'd be a pariah. I have to tough this out."

A call came in: domestic disturbance at an apartment building across town. Sandy flipped on lights and siren. Mack hated family fights. Cops and innocent bystanders sometimes died when passions flew out of control. He focused on the matter at hand and hoped this would not be one of those times.

***

By three o'clock, Little Miss Kindergarten had returned, shared her grilled cheese sandwich with Mommy, and enjoyed a good nap. The other two were descending the bus steps. Grandma—Mack's mother—waited in the living room to take her three favorite kidlings to her house for a sleepover, their first. Since Honey forbade overnights, feeling the children were still a little young, Marla had asked no questions and turned up an hour early. Just as Honey finished checking the tracking online again.

Honey sat on the edge of her chair, fidgeting and keeping an eye on the picture window behind her mother-in-law's broad silhouette. The bus doors closed, and the yellow vehicle pulled away with a whoosh. Leaping to her feet, Honey herded her five-year-old and the older woman toward the door. She'd piled the overnight bags and toys in the car when Marla arrived.

"Okay, you might as well go. Thanks for taking the kids, Mom. You know how much they enjoy visiting with you and Dad." By intercepting the other two, she could prevent the inevitable time loss. Although she'd packed their special toys and electronics, if Bonnie and Eric got in the house, they'd dally, and she couldn't afford to waste so much time.

Not with her last peek at the online order tracking showing the item expected anytime.

"Okay, everyone, hop in the car." She reached in to check seat belts and kiss foreheads. "Grandma needs to get going."

Marla slid behind the wheel, muttering. "I'm not sure what the rush is."

"Rush hour, Mom. I know how you hate it."

"Where will I encounter a traffic jam in the two miles of suburbia between our homes?"

Honey closed the driver's door. "Have a great time, everyone. Be good for Grandma and Grandpa." Desperation rose as a big truck turned the corner. "Bye now." Leave! If a box arrived, her nosy mother-in-law would get out of the car to watch her open it. What a horrifying scenario.

To her relief, Marla put the car in gear and backed out, shaking her head. The woman likely doubted her sanity, but better that than the alternative.

Sure enough, the truck groaned to a stop in front of her home and the driver hopped out, a big box cradled in his muscular arms. He headed up her walk. "Delivery."

A master of understatement.

"Thanks." The plain brown cardboard gave nothing away, but she blushed anyway. "I'll take it."

He eyed her. "I can take it inside for you if you like."

She blushed harder. "Oh, no, it's not heavy is it?"

"Nope, what is it? Candles or something?" He passed her the package and smiled. "I know how you ladies like your pretty things."

Honey nodded. "Yeah. We all like our candles and things." Taking a step back, she wished him into the truck. "Well, thanks."

"Sure thing. Hey, you look kind of flushed. Maybe you'd better get out of the sun."

The man would never leave. "Oh, good idea. Thanks again." Sure she'd achieved cheeks the color of ripe cherries, Honey fled into the cool darkness of the foyer and closed the door with a firm click. True to her profession, she had a practical, calculating streak a mile wide. Her clothes, her organization even with her family reflected this. When Marla opened those overnight bags, she would find neatly folded necessities. The chances of her needing to come back for anything were virtually nil.

Except... Honey's eyes lit on a capacious, black leather tote on the floor next to the coffee table. Dammit! Marla did not share her daughter-n-law's sense of organization. *And I did push her out the door.* Her fist closed around the handle, her heart sinking into her belly. No doubt the older woman's cell phone lay inside as well, so she couldn't even call her to come back.

A loud honk out front sent her flying to fling the door open, bag still clutched in her hand. *Thank God.* She hurried down the walk and thrust the purse through the open window.

"It's your fault, you hurried me so. I couldn't believe it when I—"

Relief mingling with impatience forced Honey to smile and nod. "You're right, Mom. I'm glad you noticed right away." She blew kisses toward the backseat. "Don't unbuckle those seat belts. Bye now." Before Marla could say another word—which could have begun an interminable story of the last time or six she'd left her bag somewhere—Honey dropped the purse on the passenger seat and made a beeline for the house. Rude, maybe, but she had no time to waste. After a moment, the car pulled away with only a slight screech of tires to indicate the driver's opinion of her attitude.

Honey had always stayed to listen, no matter how familiar the tale. The dutiful daughter-in-law showed respect to her husband's parents. No rocking the boat.

But the same nature held her back in the bedroom, kept her from initiating anything new with Mack. A situation she was about to change.

She grabbed a knife and plopped the carton on the kitchen island. Drawing a deep breath, she slit the tape and opened Pandora's box.

Piles of glittery violet tissue paper filled the container, and Honey dug through it, tossing the crumpled sheets aside as she hunted for the answer to all their problems in the bedroom. At the bottom of the box, she found a lavender and black patterned drawstring bag about the size of one of Mack's socks and pulled it out. Loosening the tie, she reached inside and froze. Honey darted over to the kitchen window and jerked the frilly curtains closed.

Back at the counter, she opened the bag and spilled the contents into her hand. Biting her lip, she examined the clear cup with a mini-vibrator inside and plastic tubing. It connected to a small device with two batteries taped to the back. The whole thing terrified her.

When ordering it, the fright had been fun, like a quick scare in a movie. She'd envisioned herself powdered and perfumed and laid out on the bed in a sexy negligee like a 1950s starlet, her hair cascading over her shoulders in soft shiny waves. She would smile and say, "You're home, darling. Come see what I bought us."

If she had this much trouble even looking at a pussy pump, how on earth would she use it in front of Mack? What if she did it wrong? Sexy could go to awkward or worse fast—making her fix to their problem a disaster.

Honey picked up the device and marched for the bedroom. She'd have to try it first, on her own. Worst-case scenario, it might not fit or wouldn't have any effect. Since her purchase consisted of a small pump mechanism and a suction cup, an unpromising and unsexy gizmo, if it didn't work, she'd prepare a candlelight dinner to set a romantic mood anyway. They would be alone, and if Mack didn't fall asleep right after they ate, she could try to coax him into an early bedtime. No earthshaking changes, but at least a longer session and some uninterrupted time together.

Dropping the pump on the dresser, she headed for the shower then changed her mind. A bath might relax her, and a bubble bath even more. With hours before Mack's return, she sank up to her neck in a sea of milky foam, her tense neck muscles relaxing. Her handsome husband would appreciate the gesture and, in her fairytale imagination, be so wowed by her daring, they'd have a night like they used to. Making love in every position possible. She might even consider that way. Desperate times called for desperate actions.

Rubbing the sponge over her breasts and down her stomach, she frowned at the faint white stretch marks. She wouldn't trade her imps for anything, not even the smooth, flat belly she'd once been so proud of. Mack told her he treasured her body more since it gave birth to the three, and she believed him. She couldn't have picked a kinder, more loving father if she'd had the whole world to choose from. When he sat next to his eldest going over her homework or lifted the baby in his strong arms to hug her, Honey's heart thumped.

What a package.

The bubbles dissipated. Squeaky clean, she would have to approach the dragon on the dresser. She shouldn't be frightened of the pussy pump. The device guaranteed to put the zip back in their relationship. Stepping out of the tub, she reached for a towel and wrapped it around her body, patting herself dry, distressed by the shake in her hand.

C'mon, Honey. If it doesn't work out, he'll never even know. And if it does, it might be the answer.

She hung the towel on a hook and picked up the pump on her way to the bed. Lying on her back, she held the suction cup over her naked, defenseless pussy. Could it be worse than waxing? "Okay, so what do we do here?" Instructions would have been helpful. Honey inserted the batteries in the black box and pressed the plastic cup to her skin, a little alarmed when it covered her entire slit, stopping short of her anus. She was pretty sure she didn't want to make that swell—she'd never encouraged play in that area. If it looked too alluring, Mack might think she'd changed her mind, and she wasn't sure yet she had.

Holding the device in place, she lifted the box with her other hand and gave a tentative push to the button. Nothing happened so she squeezed harder and the hard plastic edges dug in. Honey let go of the suction cup, and it stayed in place.

She flicked the switch from low to medium. Heat gathered in her pubic region. Not like normal arousal, like when Mack stroked her or rubbed her clit. Almost a burning. A little concerned, she turned it on high, determined to get maximum benefit from her purchase. What would she look like when she finished? Irresistable, as the website claimed? Guaranteed to drive her lover crazy with passion? Rather reminded her of those collagen injections women got to make their mouths look "bee stung." All the fashion magazines at the grocery checkout called the effect super sexy, but she had her doubts.

Focused on the intriguing sensations between her legs, she let the pump run for several minutes. A tingling followed the warmth, her captive pussy reacting to the pressure in a most positive way. A dull thrum of arousal responded to the cleverly built-in vibrator buzzing over her clit. The next best thing to hands-free eroticism. Honey's lower belly tightened and she flicked the switch, turning the device off. She'd never intended to orgasm with the thing, not without Mack. She'd bought it for the sole purpose of adding excitement and another level of intimacy to their marriage. Maybe even a little fun. But not for solo fun.

She set the box on the bed, expecting the plastic cup to fall away, but the mighty pump with its powerful suction had created some kind of hermetic seal. The dang thing refused to come loose.

Honey pried at the edges with her fingernails, trying to get it off without gouging her skin, but the evil torture device still stayed, stuck. Cursing under her breath, she slipped off the bed and waddled, spraddle-legged to the kitchen, the black box dangling down her thigh, to paw through the carton. Perhaps she'd missed some sort of instruction sheet in her hurry to grab the prize.

No way would Mack find her sexy like this. He couldn't even see if her lips were swollen and sensual. Instead of a romantic interlude, she'd created a situation likely to end in a trip to the emergency room. How humiliating. Even if she got it off, the whole process of lying on the bed while a suction cup stuck to her pussy and a small machine hummed might not be the solution to her marital blahs. Unless it gave Mack other ideas....

The deep-purple tissue went flying as she dug to the bottom, but no helpful paperwork surfaced. In a burst of frustration, she tossed the container to the floor. Maybe she should call a plumber to get the evil device off her pubic area, which throbbed in a less pleasant way. Panic sent tingles of adrenalin through her arms and legs.

Without warning, for reasons of its own, the suction cup released and fell to the floor between her feet. Panting with relief, she picked it up and turned the cardboard box upright. Honey scooped up the fallen tissue paper and shoved it back where it came from. To the trash with you. I'll have to run to the store and get something special to prepare for our candlelight dinner. Heading for the back door, she kicked an object on the floor. What on Earth? When she scooped it up, she found a lavender plastic bag marked "Free with Purchase."

Despite her disenchantment with the pump—and the irritated, still-warm sensation in her labia—Honey's curiosity rose. A freebie.... She left the box on the floor and returned to the counter where she unzipped the bag and dumped the contents into her palm.

Oh, shit no. She held either her worst nightmare or the answer to her prayers. Shifting from foot to foot as her still-puffy lips made their presence known, Honey closed her fist around what her research taught her was a butt plug. Made of blue plastic, a few inches long and with a teardrop shape, the device narrowed to a blunted top then narrowed to flare again into a wide flange at the bottom with a finger grip. A beginner's model, so made to prevent nasty accidents where things disappeared inside a person.

Her research on Sodom&Gomorrah.com left her quite knowledgeable about the devices, although she'd rejected the idea of buying one. Still...with the pussy pump out of the question for the evening, desperation ruled her mind. Mack wanted to try anal play. He'd said so more than once, although he'd never pushed the issue.

Maybe trying out the shiny blue toy would help her adjust to the idea. Not very big. Not much larger than his thumb. And he would be so pleased.

The S&G product page had been quite clear about the need for lube in any kind of anal play, but another search of the box showed no sign of any helpful tubes or jars. Honey glanced at the clock. She still had at least an hour before Mack returned home. The poor man had been pulling overtime every day for two weeks. She had plenty of time to run to the drugstore for lube and still go to grocery store for something special for his dinner.

Feeling like wife of the year, Honey started for the bedroom to dress. She winced when a sudden movement rubbed her pussy lips together. Still swollen—but how long could it last? Did her reaction compare to a man's erection? If so, as soon as arousal wore off, so would the swelling. Of course, the man's cock had not been subjected to a vacuum device...but wouldn't the principle be the same?

She trailed a finger over her labia and jumped. So sensitive. Her eyes drifting closed, she rubbed some more, pausing to circle her clit for good measure. If it would reduce the puffiness, perhaps an orgasm was a good idea. Adding a second finger, she glided back and forth, amazed at her wetness. So good.

Mack couldn't mind her doing this, for the sake of being able to leave the house…could he?

She leaned against the dresser, speeding up her motions, picturing Mack on his knees between her legs. When they had time, he had the tongue of a god, lapping at her pussy with untiring enthusiasm until she spilled her juices in orgasm. Then he licked on, nibbling at the sensitive clit, sliding fingers inside her like…yes, ohhh.

Mmmm. Honey held the image in her mind, remembering how he would wrap his arms around her, hold her tight so she couldn't wriggle away when she became too sensitive. He parted her lips and sucked her clit into his mouth, working it there….

Oh, Mack! Her knees buckled, and she fell into a crouch with the power of her orgasm. Even in her imagination, only her husband could drive her to those heights. Chills chased over her skin.

Whew. What would it be like when Mack got home? Maybe she could use the pump with him sometime, but not today. Because her post-orgasmic labia were no smaller than the pre-orgasmic version. How long could they stay in their current state?

For the moment, she did not think she could bear anything against her skin. A long, wraparound denim skirt should conceal her commando status and avoid any embarrassing wardrobe malfunctions. Feeling odd, she pulled her white lacey bra from the drawer and left the matching panties behind. Honey ran a comb through her hair and dashed out to the car before she could worry about it any more. In buying lube, she made a decision.

Anal sex loomed in her future...her very near future.

Chapter Three

The domestic abuse situation turned out to be less difficult than it could have been but it did take up most of the day and require a great deal of paperwork. As happened more and more often, he and Sandy had to call another car so the battling spouses could be transported separately to jail to cool off. The new chief had a zero-tolerance policy for physical violence and not one but two parties sported black eyes. Mack pictured the wide blue eyes of his own wife and couldn't imagine putting a fist in them.

When they realized they were to be arrested, the combatants changed tactics and swore they had each walked into a wall, but their previous litany of complaints belied their new claims. Perhaps a night in jail would teach them manners or at least not to leave obvious marks.

By the time the arrest was completed and the last report filed, Mack was starving, lunchtime long past.

"Let's grab a hot dog, Sandy. My treat."

"Sounds good, as long as you don't want to continue the conversation we started earlier." Sandy flashed him a grin and punched him in the shoulder, taking some of the sting out of her comments. "Seriously, I'm sure your wife feels she scored in her choice of spouse. As well she should. You're a catch, my friend."

"You always make me feel better. I'll even spring for sauerkraut."

"What a prince. You know I hate the stuff."

But Mack didn't and the hot dog cart in the park across the street even had Michigan sauce, that beanless chili topping so dear to his New York roots. Honey would have a fit if she witnessed what he was about to eat. The veggie wrap and apple she'd made him would go uneaten. His mouth watered at the thought of the treat awaiting him and he shoved the guilt aside. Forgive me, baby. Sometimes a man's got to eat what a man's got to eat.

***

When Honey left the drugstore, she didn't dare try for a stop at the market. She'd never been aware of her pussy before, never been in such pleasurable discomfort. She wasn't sure whether she was about to come or come apart.

With home only a few blocks away, she floored the gas pedal. Shifting in her seat, clutching the steering wheel with both hands, Honey thought she'd lose her mind. She no longer cared what might happen to her as long as the throbbing stopped. Somewhere on the Internet, perhaps on the S&G site itself, there had to be a solution to her problem. A very different issue than she'd begun the day with. Why hadn't she realized how good she had it before she puffed her pussy up like a balloon?

Mack would laugh his ass off when he learned of her attempts to seduce him. So distracted by her thoughts, she sailed through a stop sign, not noticing until it was too late to react. The siren piercing her musings pushed her over the edge and she burst into tears, still fidgeting.

"License and registration, please, ma'am."

Oh no. Honey sniffed back her sobs and reached into the glove box for the registration then dug in her purse. As she pulled out the documents, the drugstore bag fell to the floor and the tube of lube rolled into view. She broke into a sweat. A cop's wife did not want to commit a crime, no matter how small. Mack had to report any infractions by his immediate family to his superior officer within twenty-four hours. Way to plan a romantic evening.

Beads of sweat trickled between her legs, further irritating her swollen tissues. She rubbed against the seat, trying for subtlety and failing.

"Ma'am, is something wrong?" The officer leaned into the car and raised a brow. "I'm afraid I have to ask you to step out of the car."

Honey cringed. She never felt more naked than when fully dressed sans panties. "Are you sure that's necessary, officer? I realize I ran a stop sign, and I am so sorry. I promise to be careful in the future." More salty droplets; she'd never noticed sweat in her girly parts before. Why now? Maybe because they were so big, catching everything like a rain gutter. When would the damn things shrink back to normal?

With their small local police force, although Honey had not met—she scanned his badge—Officer Baxter, Mack would know him. She might be able to talk him out of the ticket, but not without dropping her husband's name, and Mack would be embarrassed enough telling the chief. If this officer was a bigmouth and he realized her identity, Mack would be humiliated.

Thank heavens she'd kept her maiden name for work reasons. She'd take her medicine and make the best of it. Slipping from behind the steering wheel, Honey faced the tall, thin uniformed cop. Her pussy throbbed so hard with the motion, she feared it showed through the long, denim skirt. Smoothing the front, she checked the knot at her waist. Why she'd chosen a wraparound with no panties....

"Face the car, please."

She held her ground, resisting. "Can you tell me why?"

"You're intoxicated, and I am going to pat you down and arrest you."

Stars blanketed the blackness in front of Honey's eyes. "I'm not drunk. What gave you that idea?" This gets worse and worse.

"You can't even stand still. If you're not drunk, or under the influence of some controlled substance, what's wrong with you?"

I'm either an irresponsible drinker, about to lose my license, or...what? Sorry, Officer Baxter, I'm only a pervert. Is there a cell set aside for horny housewives who made foolish purchases online?

She took the angry road. Facing him, hands on hips, she scowled. "I have not had anything to drink stronger than coffee. I insist on a breathalyzer test." She hadn't been married to a cop for over ten years for nothing.

"It's up to you, but I still have to pat you down before I can put you in the car. Unless you want me to get a woman here to do it?"

He would have to send for Sandy, currently riding around with Mack.... "Just get it over with. I have things to do."

"Keep your pants on. You're awfully anxious to get this test." Baxter rummaged in the front seat and came up with a device about the size of a police radio with a plastic tube sticking out of the side. He pushed a series of buttons and stared at the screen. "Damn thing's on the fritz again. Piece of shit. I don't know why I even came to work in this podunk town."

Between her physical discomfort and the policeman's odd and maybe even hostile attitude, Honey's concerns grew. She tried to remember whether Mack had mentioned Officer Baxter but came up with nothing. Not good. Mack only brought home the more positive stories of the department. An issue she'd meant to discuss with him—she wished he'd share the downs as well as the ups.

It would have been helpful to know more now. "Maybe I can walk a straight line or count backward from one hundred by sevens or something?"

"People watch too much TV." The cop glowered at the device then at her. "I have to take you in, face the car." He flung the broken breathalyzer into the front seat and grabbed her forearm, fingers digging into her skin. "Now, I don't have all day."

Honey yelped and tugged at her arm. "Let go of me." She'd begun concerned about whether he'd find out she had no panties on when he patted her down, but his aggression had her unsure what he might be capable of. "My husband is Mack McGee. Let go of me right now, or you'll regret it."

His harsh laugh frightened her even more. "Mack McGee? That wuss? There's a laugh. He wouldn't harm a fly. But it would be fun to make him look bad." He spun her against the fender, the air going out of her lungs in a whoosh then placed the other hand between her shoulders and frisked her—taking a long time, rubbing his hand over her back and buttocks then up her sides so his fingers reached the edges of her breasts. Humiliated, she fought back the tears stinging her eyes.

"Do you have any weapons on you? Anything I could stab myself on?"

If only. "I don't even have any pockets. Where would I put it?"

He reached around to pat down her front, missing the nipples but not by much. His hot breath, reeking of whatever garlicky foul thing he'd had for lunch, moistened her neck. "I don't know, Mrs. Mack." He released her back and lay his full weight against her back. "I don't think pockets are the only thing you don't have on you. Maybe we could spend a little time together and make this whole ugly problem go away. So your husband isn't humiliated by a wife in jail for drinking in the afternoon."

Rage boiled over, and she thrust herself off the car, shoving him away. "If you want to arrest me, I suggest you put me in the backseat of the patrol car now, or I'm leaving."

He chuckled and grabbed her wrist, twisting her arm behind her back until she grunted with pain. Cold steel closed around one wrist then he wrestled her other arm behind her as well and locked the handcuffs in place. As she trembled, he turned her to face him and caressed her cheek. "Maybe this is what you want? I can get the lube from your car and bend you over the backseat...show you how a real man puts it to a slut."

Honey's knee shot up before she even thought about it, slamming him right where it would do the most good. "Arrest me or don't, Officer Baxter. But I promise you will regret this."

Fisting a handful of her hair, he pulled her aside, opened the car door, and shoved her in. "It's your word against mine, and we in the department look dimly on housewives who drink themselves into a dangerous state then set out to pick up their innocent children from school. Child endangerment. You're lucky I stopped you before you killed them all."

She opened her mouth to say—she had no idea what, but the slamming door would have drowned it out anyway. Protesting she was not a housewife would solve nothing. Nor would she tell him her children were at Grandma's.

"I'm taking you in under suspicion of drunken driving and on a charge of assault on a police officer. You have the right to remain silent...."

As the litany droned on, words Honey had heard on TV crime shows but never expected to have addressed to her, hot tears slid down her cheeks. Her arms were pulled tight behind her back, and she wriggled, trying to take some of the painful strain from her shoulders with no success. But the discomfort held nothing compared to the trepidation crawling up her spine at what her well-intentioned actions had led to for Mack.

Baxter patted his pocket and pulled out a cigarette and lighter. "It's a shame we couldn't have handled the situation before it got this far. Your husband will never hear the end of it. And isn't he in line for a promotion?" He flicked the lighter, drew in a deep drag, and blew it out through his nose. "He can kiss his stripes good-bye."

Mack's sweet face flashed through her mind, the tired lines by his eyes deepened by working long hours every day and studying at night, proud of his ability to take care of his family. Her income went to extras, vacations, and the kids' college accounts. They lived on one income and saved for the future.

And because his supposedly intelligent wife suffered a ditzy moment of insecurity, he would lose it all. The promotion had become the least of their concerns. Could he lose his job over her stupidity? The respect of his co-workers would dissipate like smoke.

Wriggling again to find a comfortable position, a horrific thought suppressed the others. Swallowing hard she choked out the question. "Am I going to be processed and put in a cell?" Strip-searched? Those words would not come out.

"It's not too late to accept my offer. Nothing's in writing." Baxter dropped the butt and ground it out with his shoe. When she didn't respond, he climbed in the car and smiled over his shoulder, long incisors reminding her of the wolf in Red Riding Hood. And he'd gobble her up, given half a chance. Damned if she would provide it. Mack's career was one thing, and she'd do a lot to protect it, but his family was another and the bad cop in the front seat would destroy them. It would kill her husband to find out she'd traded her virtue for a get-out-of-jail-free card. Not that she could allow Baxter to touch her without vomiting.

"Drive on, officer." She settled back, wincing as the muscles in her arms twinged in protest. "We'll settle it downtown." Honey forced back tears again, not wanting to give him the satisfaction. She had a little pride left yet—at least until some beefy prison matron got a look at her distorted parts and called 9-1-1.

Chapter Four

"**B**est hot dog I've had in a long time." Mack tossed the paper napkin in a nearby trash bin and rose from the park bench he'd occupied for the past ten minutes. "I enjoyed the extra-spicy mustard."

"Right." Sandy elbowed him and headed back toward the station. "I believe it was the first one you've had in a while. Ever since Honey started packing you those healthy lunches."

He fell in next to her. "She swears if I don't start taking better care of myself, I'll end up with a heart condition like my dad."

"She's right." His partner's tone lost its joviality and became serious. "You're lucky to have a woman who loves you so much and takes such good care of you. I like being single sometimes, not having to answer to anyone...but other times it would be nice to have someone around who cares."

"Sandy, don't go soft on me. But you know I care. Juanita, too. And the chief. Most of the guys, too. Even if they do flirt too hard, sometimes."

"I appreciate your friendship, but it's not the same." She paused and rested a hand on his arm. "But since you brought it up, I've been mulling over what you said about Baxter. I think you're right." Sandy wore her hair in a long braid, and her uniform fit in a professional way, emphasizing her attractive feminine shape. But he rarely thought of her as a woman. His partner, his right hand, a cop. Someone he could depend on in a crisis.

Yet, because of her femininity, she suffered unfair treatment, treated as an object by one of their fellow officers. If anyone behaved toward Honey in such a rude manner, he wouldn't be responsible for his actions.

"How about if I come with you to talk to the chief?" He headed across the street, and she fell in beside him again. "Help explain what's going on and your concerns. He's a good man. He'd never let one of his officers be harassed."

"Chief O'Reilly is not a man to listen to concerns in a placid way." Sandy laughed. "He'll blow his stack. Everyone within a hundred yards will know what he's yelling about. Why do you think I've held out so long?"

He sighed. "Hang in there. I'm sure we can come up with a solution besides beating the crap out of Baxter—even if knocking his block off would be the most logical solution."

"Castration would be my choice for him. I can't be the first one he pulled his despicable behavior on. I will control myself for now, but if we can't figure it out soon, I'll have to start applying to other departments. I hear Bonneville has some openings, and Hastings."

"Don't even consider leaving." Ideas raced through his head. "Honey sat on a grievance committee before she started telecommuting. She'll have some ideas. I'm sure of it. Let me speak with her tonight and then we will reassess...or maybe you can come over this weekend?"

"I don't want to bother her, Mack. She's so busy with the kids and work and everything."

He slapped her on the shoulder, feeling better. "She likes you, Sandy, and she knows how valuable a good partner is. It's settled. You come over tomorrow afternoon, and we'll throw some burgers on the grill, and then after the kids go to bed we can sit down and fix everything."

"Mack, you have such faith in your wife, I almost believe it's possible. Okay, I promise I won't quit or shoot Baxter before Saturday. Then, I make no promises."

"Deal." Honey would fix it. If she could make him a better man, after his youthful tendencies to be irresponsible and enjoy the suds too much, she could do anything. More at peace, he strolled into the station and up to the front desk.

Juanita, sitting off to the side, gestured them over. "Mack, before you head out on patrol again, there's something you need to know. Sandy, you stick around, too. This concerns a problem I've seen you trying to deal with as well."

***

Honey huddled on the bunk in the corner of the small cell, shivering. Did they have to keep the air conditioning so low? Her clothes did not offer much warmth and a draft ran right up her skirt. Although that soothed her pussy. It had begun to subside, a little, but she was still hyperaware of it.

She had Juanita to thank for the privacy, at least. Baxter had tried to have her tossed in the drunk tank, but the female officer held firm, escorting her to the solo space after the most cursory of pat downs and a quick puff on a working breathalyzer showing no blood alcohol. Her lack of respect for the arresting officer showed in her tight lips and the crinkle between her eyes, but she only said, "I'll get Mack as soon as possible. Baxter's crossed the line this time," before closing the door behind her.

The hollow clang would haunt Honey's nightmares for the rest of her days. The sound heralded the end of Mack's career. He'd never be able to show his face again. They would have to move, if he could find a job on any force once word got out about his jailbird wife. And the kids.... In a small town, gossip traveled fast.

They'd have to move far away. Maybe to another state.

Due to the sensitive nature of her own work, she'd have to report her arrest to her employers as well...at least once she had her day in court. Was resisting arrest a felony? She didn't know, for sure, but she did know a felony would cost her her job.

All because she wanted to put a little spice into their love life, be the sexy woman he married instead of the worn-out wife and mother she'd become.

"Hey, there." Depression fled, replaced by rage and she dug her nails into her hands to keep from flying across the room and scratching the eyes out of the despicable face peering through the small window in the door. "You look pretty sad in there. Sorry you didn't take me up on my little offer before?"

She swallowed hard. "Don't you have better things to do than taunting the prisoners?"

"Aww, don't be like that. You know, I haven't finished the paperwork yet. I can still go easy on you." He leered, showing nicotine-stained teeth. She fought her gag impulse. "Want to change your mind?"

Honey wrapped her arms around her legs, hugging them close to her. Her bravado simmered under the surface, as if she stood a chance of doing something in retaliation. His word against hers. Even if Mack didn't believe him—and she didn't think he would—others would.

"Stay right there." She stood up and strode to the window, ready to share her opinion of his character without reservation when she saw a flicker of motion behind him. In his lecherous stupor, he must not have noticed. Hope lit in her breast, and she stood tall again. "So, Officer Baxter, before I turn you down again, maybe you'd better tell me what you propose. Can you really keep from charging me?"

He winked, and a gust of garlicky breath with an undertone of old cigarettes and coffee touched her face. She fought the urge to cringe away and instead turned her lips up in what she hoped resembled a sexy smile.

"All you have to do is be friendly. Once we complete our little agreement, I will see to it you get out, no harm no foul. A failure to complete the paperwork should do it."

She batted her eyes. "You can let me out with no charges? You have so much power?"

"Oh you'd be amazed what I can do. Last month, I had a similar situation with a lady who had, shall we say, fallen into unfortunate circumstances. After I chased her customer off, she suggested a little quality time together to clear up any misunderstandings—if you get my drift." His eyes drooped, as if he remembered something sensual and pleasant. "You know, we can take care of our little deal right now. There won't be another check of the cells for an hour. We can get real close by then. Lucky those new cameras 'broke' again this afternoon." He chuckled.

Ewww. Did he say he's taking favors from hookers? And wanted to come right in and yank off his disgusting pants to show her his gross thing? He apparently thought his tales would be, what, an incentive? She turned her head to the side and sucked in a breath of non-foul air then faced him again. Behind him, she saw Sandy's face and decided to take a chance.

"I'm so nervous." She chewed her lip, thinking. She wanted her name cleared and his ground into the mud. "So, this young woman performed some kind of favors and you let her go?"

"She sucked me off. You don't think I'd put my dick in a hooker's dirty twat do you?"

Holy shit. Hang in there, Honey, we'll take this bastard down yet. Patience. "Oh, you are smart. So you want me to ummm suck you off, too?" She'd have to wash her mouth out with strong soap after the conversation, to be able to live with herself again.

"Not you, baby. I want to fuck you silly, show you how a real cock feels. Of course, if you want, you can give me a blowjob first, show your gratitude. I wouldn't want to deny you the pleasure. In fact, since Juanita so kindly gave you a private room, I can slip right in. "

Her eyes must be bloodshot with rage, but she needed him to keep talking, so there'd be no mistake. "So, you are saying if I agree to have sex with you"— she couldn't keep using his expressions or she'd throw up—"you will drop the charges against me?"

He snorted. "Yes, if you have sex with me, I will drop all the charges." Sandy's grin appeared feral behind him. "Got it?"

"No, but I do," Sandy crowed. Baxter's howl filled the air. "Oh I'm just restraining you by twisting your arm a little bit, don't be a big baby." She giggled. "You have the right to remain silent...." Suddenly the world exploded.

A roar shook the bars and something crashed against the door. Everyone disappeared and though Honey stood on tiptoe to peer through the window, she didn't see anything.

"You bastard!" Mack! "How dare you speak to my wife like that!" A series of thuds and crashes were followed by an ominous silence. She listened, but for a long moment, nothing else happened.

Honey pounded on the door. "Mack, are you okay? Sandy? Someone let me out of here!" Her heart thumped and her breathing rasped in the silence.

Keys jingled, and the heavy door creaked open. Honey dashed into the corridor. Juanita, holding the key ring, took her arm. "Stand aside, Honey. Let the officers do their jobs."

Sandy was hauling a semiconscious Baxter to his feet. She smiled and dropped his arm and the man slithered to a heap on the floor. "Hi, Honey. Good job in there, keeping him talking. We have a solid case against him."

Mack pulled Honey into his embrace and held her tight. "Are you hurt? Did he touch you?"

"No, only talk—enough to make me gag, but he didn't do more than maybe an excessive pat down."

"I'm so sorry this happened, Honey. Will you be okay with Juanita while we take this cop-gone-bad and show the chief the footage?"

She snuggled into his welcome warmth, the shivers she'd forgotten about in all the excitement dying away. "Footage?"

"Sure, our new system records the activities in the jail constantly. The hallway and each cell."

"But he—" she kicked at the man on the floor with the toe of her shoe "—said it was broken."

Sandy laughed. "He unplugged it. We 'fixed' it and Mack has been standing outside watching the whole show."

Juanita tsked, her beehive hairdo wobbling dangerously. "I was close to cuffing your husband to keep him there as long as I did. We needed Baxter to incriminate himself."

A moan echoed from the heap at their feet. "Let's get this done with, Mack, so you can take Honey home."

Chapter Five

Driving Honey Home.

Her car sat in the impound lot, but it could wait. There would be no fees. And no charges against Honey. The chief had wanted to extend his apologies for his officer—former officer's—behavior, but Mack requested he hold off while she recovered from her stint in jail. Baxter had been placed on leave without pay while Internal Affairs reviewed the evidence against him. His detention handled Sandy's worries as well, without them ever having to be aired. With the footage from the jail corridor and his car—the dumbass hadn't realized even if he stood out of camera range the microphone recorded his every word—his firing and criminal charges awaited.

Mac signaled and pulled into their driveway as dusk darkened the neighborhood. "What a long day."

"Mmm, yes." Honey sat, unmoving, until he came around, unfastened her seat belt, and helped her to her feet.

"Are you sure you're okay?" He gaped. "Honey, I forgot about the kids! They are all alone and...."

She waved a hand in the air. "At your mother's house for the night."

"Oh, you used your call to take care of them. Dear God, what does Mom think happened?" He wrapped an arm around her waist and guided her up the sidewalk and inside.

She pulled away and set her purse on the entry table. "I'm fine. You don't have to treat me like glass. And Marla doesn't think anything. They left with her before I went to the store, when all this happened."

Mack took a step back and eyed her. "What did happen? Of course, the chief assured me there will be no charges against you, not after Baxter's behavior."

"And somehow the camera didn't work again while you attempted to take Baxter into custody." She giggled, looking more herself, and his tight shoulders relaxed a little.

"Coincidence. But I want to know—"

Honey rose on tiptoe and pressed a soft kiss to his lips. "And you have a right to know. But I would love to take a bath and go to bed. If you don't mind?"

He mentally kicked himself as Honey slipped into the bathroom and the rush of water filled his ears. After the day she'd had, his wife deserved kindness and gentle care. She'd come within inches of being raped by that bastard. Rage rose again, heating his face. He hadn't had enough time to express his feelings, even if Baxter had ended up with two black eyes and a split lip while "trying to escape." At least one of those injuries came from Sandy's small but efficient fists. She'd glowed afterward, so pretty all the men in the squad room had watched her as she shoved Baxter toward the chief's office. They weren't all married and maybe....

Now he sounded like an old matchmaker. But his wife would need sustenance when she emerged from her bath. He could best help her by rustling up something for her to eat and drink in bed, waited on by her humble husband.

***

Honey rose from her second bubble bath of the day, depressed. She'd planned such a special evening. Romantic dinner—nope, no dinner at all, since she'd never made it to the store. Sex toys—shudder. Long, sweet kisses and lovemaking like long ago—no. She would crawl off to bed and try to forget the day ever happened. In the morning, she'd go get the kids and take them to the park or something. Have an ordinary day as an ordinary wife. Why had she tried to change things anyway?

The PTA ladies were right. She had a husband who wanted to have quickie morning sex with her four times a week, who kissed her good-bye and ate her healthier versions of foods he liked with minimal complaints.

And as to jealousy about Sandy...the officer had helped save Honey from Baxter and she'd be forever grateful. She'd also spilled the beans about Mack's hot dog diet cheat and promised to keep Honey informed in future. They'd bonded.

Once she had a good night's sleep, perhaps she could think of a nice man to introduce Sandy to. After all, a married partner was a less worrisome partner. Especially when the partner in question was so lovely.

Honey grabbed her old, soft terry-cloth robe from the hook and belted it around her. Enough of trying to be something she wasn't. Pussy pumps and anal plugs. Better to remember how good it was to be Mack's wife and the mother of three healthy, beautiful children. With a soft comfortable bed in her future.

But when she pulled the door open, the soft glow of a dozen candles lit the bedroom. A battered tray sat in the middle of the bed with a bottle of wine, two glasses, and some crackers spread with...peanut butter?

"I wish it was fancier. We're out of those tiny cheese ball things you like."

Honey brushed tears away as she walked toward her hero, still in his police uniform, with the shirt rumpled and a rip in the sleeve. He had a scrape over his eye and she lifted on tiptoe to kiss it. "You're the most wonderful man." The weight of the day overwhelmed her. Sobs shaking her shoulders, she buried her face in his chest. His arms tightened around her waist and she cried until she couldn't cry anymore.

"It's only peanut butter."

Laughter replaced the tears. She sniffed. "I know, but it's peanut butter and candles and you."

Mack stroked her back and murmured nonsense until the hysteria faded, to be replaced by a smooth calm. When she lay limp against him, he scooped her up, one arm under her knees, and laid her on the bed. "Baby, are you sure you're okay? What happened to my calm, practical wife?"

She lifted her arms to him, but he waved her away. "Give me a minute to shower and change. You smell so sweet and good and I'm all sweaty from work." Sweaty or dirty or covered in mud made little difference. But he disappeared before she could protest, and Honey lay back to wait. He didn't take long and in a moment returned, his hair slicked back and a towel around his waist.

"Mack?" Honey shrugged her robe from her shoulders.

"Yes?" He dropped the towel and stood naked in front, his erection proud in front of him.

She lifted her arms again and this time he didn't resist. Mack knelt on the bed, unknotted the belt, and parted the robe, baring her. She looked her fill at his body, realizing she'd not had the chance to admire his manliness in a while. Their quickies took place under the covers or in the shadows of early morning. Often she drifted, still in a half dream while he made love to her.

She took in every inch of the man she'd married, glad to have the chance to learn his new contours with her eyes instead of by touch. The reddish-blond hair on his forearms and the sprinkling on his chest caught the light of the bedside lamps. His shoulders were, if anything, broader than she remembercd, strong and able to bear the responsibiliy of their family. To hold her close and let her release her worries. A good reminder. Sometimes she kept things to herself, not wanting to burden him after his long days fighting crime, but in holding back, she did him a disservice.... Did her reticence make him unwilling to share his own concerns? If she were more open, she might have learned about Baxter and been more prepared.

Mack reached over her and poured ruby-red wine into a tumbler with cartoon super heroes circling the rim. She giggled. "You couldn't find the wine glasses?"

"I can never find anything in this house," he grumbled, but grinned at her. "That's why I need you."

She pushed herself up on pillows and accepted the drink. "For no other reason?"

Mack flopped beside her. "Well, you do the laundry, too, and the cooking and shopping and...."

Honey raised an eyebrow at him and took a sip from her glass.

He smiled at her, his eyes heavy-lidded but sparkling. "I need you for everything, you know. I wouldn't be me without you."

She traced his cheek, the five-o'clock shadow scratchy under her palm. "And I need you. The kids are wonderful. They are my life. But I need more time with you, Mack. Just you and me."

He leaned into her touch, breath warm against her hand. "But you don't like to send the kids to my mom's overnight and yours is too far away."

Honey snuggled closer and pressed her lips to his, a soft brush. "Your mother drives me a little crazy—no don't argue, you know she does." She rubbed their noses together and giggled. "But she loves them, and they adore her. I am guilty of being an overprotective mama."

Mack set his glass on the night table and did the same with hers. "I love the way you take care of our family, including me, but I would welcome more evenings alone with you, and nights, and mornings. Mom will keep them safe." He kissed her, long and slow, the way he used to. No rush, no clock ticking or little people about to barge in. When they drew back to breathe, he smiled, his eyes alight with mischief. He pulled open a night table drawer and pulled out a lumpy package. Wrapped in lavender tissue paper and tied with a big purple bow. "I bought you something, well for both of us."

Oh God...I recognize the paper.

She shook it then looked from the item to her husband. "What is it? Please don't let it be another pussy pump.

"Unwrap it and see. And don't laugh."

Laughter, no. Her still slightly swollen parts gave a twinge. "Okay, sure." She grabbed the end of the ribbon but he stilled her hand.

"If you don't like it, if it isn't your thing, we can throw it away—it's not returnable. But I thought, well, I was waiting for a time when we had a few hours together." He dropped his arm to his side. "Open it."

Flicking her gaze from him to the parcel, she tugged on the ribbon and the paper parted. A trio of containers fell in her lap. She lifted one and read the label. "Warming oil?" Relief sent warmth through her limbs.

"I thought you might like a massage, a sexy one. The site said it was their bestseller. And I wanted to do something special for you." He frowned. "What did you expect?"

She squirmed, remembering her plan to be more open, communicate. "I shopped at Sodom&Gomorrah.com, too."

He stared at her. "You did? What did you buy?"

Her courage fading, Honey opened one of the jars and sniffed. "Mmm, lavender and sandalwood. I do want a massage. Can you do it now?"

Mack shook his head. "Not until you tell me what you bought. Where is it? Oh, you didn't buy one of those vibrator things did you? Honey, don't I make you come when we make love? I know it's rushed, but you seem to...."

She laid a finger over his lips. "Shhh. No I didn't buy a vibrator. And you always give me pleasure. I bought a...."

"Why won't you tell me?" His face held such distress, she blurted it out.

"A pussy pump."

His jaw dropped. "A what? Is it what I think it is?"

She nodded, face burning. "Probably."

"What does it do?"

She winced and parted her legs. "It's gone down now, but...."

"Oh, Honey!" He bent low and examined her. "Actually this is pretty sexy. What does it do, make you more sensitive?"

She nodded. "Yes, it made me so horny I...."

"You couldn't wait?" Mack began to chuckle. "Honey, you never cease to amaze me."

"You aren't mad?"

"I'd rather take care of you myself, but I understand there were extenuating circumstances."

She swallowed hard. "Then I decided I would surprise you so I dashed off to the store, assuming the swelling would go down. I was pretty freaked out."

"You mean it was more swollen than now? And you had to go to the store right then? What for? An ice pack?"

On a roll, but still embarrassed, she muttered, "There was a gift with purchase, and I needed something."

"Judging from your expression, the 'gift with purchase' has to be something special."

The humor of the situation found its way to her brain and she joined him in laughter. "Yeah, you're going to love this."

He hugged her. "Okay, baby, tell me. This is turning into one interesting night."

Honey snuggled closer and spilled the story, from when she first got the idea to making plans to ditch the children for the night, all the way up to when she ran the stop sign.

When she got to the part about Baxter, Mack tensed and held her so tight she gasped. "If I hadn't already decked him, if he weren't up on charges, I'd—"

Honey kissed him and ended his statement. Enough of the day—time to take advantage of the night. His warm lips parted, and he tugged her on top of him, straddling his waist. His cock poked at her thigh, but for once no sense of urgency enveloped her. She wriggled, enjoying his hardness, her blood flowing slow and sure through her veins.

Had it been like this before the kids? Maybe not. Their younger incarnations hadn't appreciated the gift of long, sensuous nights. Giving herself over to their kiss, she enjoyed her position of control. For some reason, girl-on-top happened rarely with her take-charge cop husband. Possibilities filled her mind while she parted her lips, inviting his tongue to play. Lost in a sensual dream, she rested her hands on his chest, digging her fingers into the solid muscle. Mack's upper body ruled, the strength of his arms one of his sexiest features. She caressed up his shoulders and down his arms, enjoying relearning his body.

Breaking their kiss, Honey nuzzled the base of his throat and crept backward, smiling when his eyes widened. "Sweetie, you don't have to...."

"Oh, but I want to." She arrived at her target and wrapped her hand around his cock. Long, hard, and smooth. "It's been a while." Honey licked her lips and winked at him. "I want to make you feel so good."

He shivered. "You always make me feel good, but, baby, turn it around. If you're going to go after my stuff with your hot mouth, I want to do the same for you. And get a closer look at your puffed-up pussy."

She blushed but didn't argue. If it had been a while since she'd blown him, it had been twice as long since he'd returned the favor. He offered, but time.... "Oh, God, yes." After a little maneuvering, she lay in classic sixty-nine, girl-on-top. Her absolute favorite position. Mack's warm breath on her sensitive pussy nearly sent her into an instant climax, but she counted back from one hundred by sevens—darn, it was hard—and calmed down enough to focus on the blunt head in front of her face. She took it into her mouth and held still for a moment, enjoying his groan.

"Go slow, baby. We have all night."

She giggled, and his cock jerked in her mouth. All night. Sweet, sweet words. But they weren't twenty anymore, and once he came, they'd have to take a break. Slow buildup led to big orgasms—and she wanted him to have the biggest. To blow his mind as well as his penis. With restraint in mind, Honey sucked on the head and slipped backward then took in a little more and licked what she had so far. In and out, deeper each time until he bumped against the back of her throat. Her cue to gag and back off—but not this time. Not with Mack's tongue drawing circles around her clit. Slow...slow...a finger gliding into her pussy and out again, in time with Honey's motions. A rhythm all their own.

Two fingers inside her then one disappeared and while Mack mouthed her pussy hard, the missing digit bumped against the rosette of her ass. Honey gasped and choked. She tensed to jerk away then relaxed. I planned to use the butt plug and maybe try out that playground anyway. A finger can't be too bad. He rubbed around and around, prodding at the tight muscle. It's pretty good. More than good. She tried to hold back but his lips, tongue, and teeth nibbling at her, added to the fingers in her pussy and ass sent her flying hard. Muscled clenched around the intrusions, and Honey covered her own teeth with her lips to avoid biting him in her bucking, jerking climax.

She sucked hard, his cock in her mouth part of the insane pleasure of her orgasm. Drew harder until he reached down and lifted her head from his cock.

"Wait, I want to come inside you. I want more. I want everything. Oh, Honey."

She released him and stayed sprawled there, her dripping pussy still over his chin. God, when had she come so hard her teeth had rattled and her heart banged in her ears? Never.

Too limp to move, yet already starting to climb again from his stubble scraping her oversensitive tissues. She would come again, but she wasn't going to be doing any of the work. Her legs and arms were overcooked spaghetti, and she rolled onto the bed when Mack sat up.

"Had enough?" He leered at her, pleasure in his deep-brown eyes. The man knew what he'd done to her, and he liked it. Of course, so did she.

"Mmm, no, but you have to be on top this time." She parted her legs. "Take me, husband."

"Anything for my wife." Mack knelt between her knees and stroked his cock. Was there anything sexier? Her libido lurched from half simmer to full boil, and a trickle of moisture tickled her thigh. Desire clouded her thoughts, desire to give him whatever he wanted, something to equal what he'd given her.

"I want to try anal." There, she'd said it, and his jaw fell open, so he'd heard. His hand stopped moving on his erection.

"Don't joke."

"Mack, my amazing hero husband, I trust you with everything I am. Including, on this special occasion, my butt."

He chuckled, but it cut off when he held her gaze. "I want to, but I don't want to hurt you."

"If it feels anything like what you did with your finger a few moments ago, I want to try."

He toyed with one of her nipples, almost absently. "Honey, you don't have to do this. You always said no before."

"That was then. When we were hurried people with five minutes for sex." She kissed the top of his head. "Now we're wild lovers, with endless time to explore our fantasies." A sudden thought occurred to her. "Crap. You know I told you I went out to the store? I got lube—my gift with purchase was a butt plug."

"And you were going to try it?" He nipped at her breast and laughed when she squeaked. "I believed you allowed the anal play because of my fabulous pussy-eating ability. A reward."

She yanked on a lock of his short hair. "It is. I only planned to try the plug. Not give you the whole enchilada."

He beamed up at her. "You have such a turn of phrase. But I am not a completely stupid man, and if you are willing to reward my heroism with the coveted ass trophy, who am I to say no?"

"But we can't. I went to the store because I didn't get any lube with the plug."

He arched a brow. "And?"

"And the lube is in my car...in the impound lot. We can't do anal without lube. Even I know that."

Mack snickered and pointed to the bottles he'd handed her earlier. "Honey, I also got a gift with purchase."

"You mean?" She watched as he lifted one of the containers.

"Yep, extra slick for your pleasure."

The pause for discussion had eroded a little of her bravado, but the eager expression on his face lent determination. And, she realized, they'd shared more in one evening than in the busy weeks and years of recent memory. Banter and open, honest conversation. Love for her husband overwhelmed any doubts. "Then I guess I'm all yours."

She rolled onto all fours and Mack piled pillows under her stomach. "Comfortable?"

"So far." Her heart thudded in her chest. "Don't take too long, or I may lose my nerve."

His broad hands rubbed her back in long, soothing strokes. "Say stop anytime."

She nodded as he moved down to massage her buttocks, digging his fingers in. His touch disappeared then a cool sensation made her jump. The lube. It dripped over her buttocks and chilled her, but to her surprise, when he worked a finger into her ass, she shuddered with lust. He pulled it out and pushed two in then spread them apart and back together, in and out, slow and steady, over and over. Honey arched her back, thrusting toward him.

"If you're ever going to do it...do it now." She tensed as the fingers retreated, to be replaced by a slippery cock.

"Now works for me." Mack gripped her waist and held her steady. "Oh, Honey." He pushed inside, the muscles tightening around his dick. "So...tight." His fingers dug into her sides, but she focused on the fullness in her ass, and when she pushed back again, he moved, deeper then out almost all the way. On the way in again, he brought one hand under her and tickled her clit. Her knees buckled, the mound of pillows holding her hips off the bed. She rode the waves, deep pleasure, stretching fullness, slight sting on the way in...and her swelling clit under his touch.

"Mack, yes, right there. Don't stop." Her hips bucked, spinning galaxies of stars obscuring her vision. She shrieked and flew over the edge into darkness as the hot liquid of his cum filled her ass, burning, but so good. So, so good.

Not like before, when they were first married. They hadn't understood each other so well then. Their night together showed her how they'd grown together, and she thanked everything in heaven for her husband and family. For a love her younger self could never have dreamed of.

Mack balanced over Honey, exhausted, muscles screaming with tension, but he wouldn't crush her with his greater weight. He didn't want to pull out though. Not yet. He wanted to stay connected to her a while longer, as close as possible. Her caramel-colored hair hung damp over her shoulders and her head rested on a cradle of her arms. She breathed long and slow.

Mack slipped away and cleaned up in the restroom then brought a damp cloth and washed Honey as well before returning to bed.

His Honey, his wife, so precious to him. She'd come into harm's way during the afternoon. He'd been there for her—and for his partner, but what if he hadn't been? One bad cop could cause so much harm. Baxter had admitted to taking favors from prostitutes, but what had stopped him from putting the moves on other women in the community? Had they buckled under the pressure? The IA investigation would take a long time, and every cop on the force would come under increased scrutiny as a result. So be it. Whatever it took to keep the citizens safe, even from those sworn to protect them.

But for now, his family and his partner were safe. Honey curled into a ball and breathed long and slow. She needed her rest, but Mack planned to wake her after a while. Even if she agreed to sending the kids to his mother's more often, they wouldn't have enough nights like this, where she could scream her passion without the pounding of tiny fists on the door.

And he wanted to make her scream again.

He yawned and stretched, pulling his wife against his chest spoon-fashion. Maybe a little nap would give him more stamina later. His eyes popped open. He'd invited Sandy for a barbecue the next day and in the chaos of the moment, he'd added in half the department. The chief was coming. Twenty people would be at their door at one in the afternoon, and Honey didn't even know she was throwing a party.

She'd be mad. He grinned and tucked her closer. But she wouldn't be mad until she knew, and he had no intention of telling her until the morning. He had plans between now and then.

How did that pussy pump work anyway?

About the Author

Kate Richards is a multi-published author of spicy romance stories in various subgenres. She lives in sunny Southern California with her wonderful husband and menagerie of rescued pets.

Kate loves the beaches, mountains and deserts of her home state as well as traveling whenever possible to meet readers and other authors.

Exploring all types of relationships in her books, Kate writes menage, BDSM, and every other kind of romance she can think of.

Also by Kate Richards

One Night on the Beach
Avalon for Christmas
The Virgin and the Playboy
The Virgin and the Best Man
Two Men and a Virgin
Gale Force Passion
Trail of Hearts
Madame Eve's Gift
Two Men
Virgin Underground
Two Dads for Christmas
The Milkman Cometh
Frontier Inferno
Lily in Chains
Terci in Chains
Sweet Christmas Kisses
All's Fair
Haunting Suspicions